THE MECHANIC'S OBSESSION

WORKING CLASS DADDIES

EMMA BRAY

CHAPTER ONE

Posh

"DAMN IT!" I exclaim before I glance over at Whitney and Jon's little girl and apologize.

"Sorry, Maggie. Don't listen to Auntie Posh."

"Damn it!" the little girl parrots. I wince.

Jon and Whitney aren't going to be happy that I'm teaching their daughter to curse, but what's a girl supposed to do when she gets stranded when she's babysitting her best friend's five-year-old daughter?

I'm not really Maggie's aunt, but seeing as

how Whitney and I don't have any blood sisters and she and I practically grew up together, what with our rich-as-sin, asshole fathers running in the same circle, we're as close to sisters as two girls can get.

Therefore, I get auntie duties.

And I love them. I do. I just fear that I totally suck at them.

I've never been what people would call a good role model. I've been called over the top and flighty, more absorbed with fashion than anything else, and I try not to let that bother me, even though there's more to me than meets the eye.

It's just easier to be a good talker and put on a show than let people close enough to see the real me. Besides, with Whitney being such a damsel in distress, one of us had to take the initiative and be the strong one.

Jon's going to skin me alive if he finds out I got stranded with his precious daughter.

Whitney's husband dotes on their daughter just as much—if not more so—than he does Whitney.

Theirs is a relationship that makes my heart ache with loneliness. I mean, I'm happy for my friend. I truly am.

But I'm a little bit jealous too.

Not that I want Jon or anything. I just want someone *like* him. Someone who sees me—the *real* me—the way he does Whitney.

But I can't think about all that now.

I have bigger problems.

Like getting my car up and running again and getting Maggie back home hopefully without Jon ever finding out what happened.

He might not ever let me babysit Maggie again if he finds out.

I bite my lip as I glance up and down the empty highway.

Shit.

Why did I have to break down in the middle of nowhere?

Okay, so it's not the middle of nowhere, but I don't see any gas stations or buildings nearby. We were on our way to the beach, and I know it's a good ten-mile trek to the nearest sign of civilization.

I look at Maggie and chew on my lip some more.

I pull out my cell phone and groan when I see that I have no service.

What am I going to do?

My eyes flick back to the road when I hear the rumble of an engine.

But it doesn't sound like a car engine.

It's a motorcycle.

My heart leaps into my chest when a man comes slowing to a stop.

Yay! We're saved! Surely, I can sweet talk this dude into helping us.

I wave and smile at him brightly, imploring words already at my lips.

But they die on my tongue when he finally reaches us and skids to a halt.

My god, this man is freaking *gorgeous*.

He has windswept, jet-black hair, a square, stubbled jawline, and aviator sunglasses that give him a hint of danger.

I'm dying to see what color his eyes are behind those shades.

He's oozing all sorts of male testosterone, and he has that bad boy vibe with his classic leather jacket, light gray tee, and ripped black jeans.

This man has managed to do something no one else in mankind has ever been able to do.

I, Jessie Cunninghman, (a.k.a. Posh) am absolutely speechless.

I can feel the heat rising in my cheeks as he dismounts and approaches us. He's tall, at least six feet. He shrugs out of his jacket, and I notice that his muscular arms are adorned with tattoos. I want to run my fingers over them, tracing the intricate designs that wrap around his biceps.

"Hey there," he says, his voice deep and rough. "Looks like you're in a bit of a predicament."

I nod dumbly, unable to form a coherent sentence.

He glances at Maggie, giving her a warm smile. "Hey, kiddo. You alright?"

"Yep! Auntie Posh is taking me to the beach!" she beams at him with all the happy obliviousness of a child.

The dude turns his attention back to me and raises an eyebrow. "Posh?"

My cheeks flame at my nickname, which suddenly seems silly. "It's what everyone calls me," I stammer, "but my real name is Jessie."

"Jessie," he says my name in a way that makes me squeeze my thighs together, though I don't know why.

His eyes flick over me and linger where my thighs are clamped tightly together.

His nostrils flare, and for some reason, that makes my pulse race. "What seems to be the problem?" he asks.

"My car broke down," I manage to stammer out. "And I don't have any cell service."

He nods, his eyes taking in my old Buick.

I see the questions in his eyes when they land back on me, and I get it. My designer clothes contradict the car I drive, but when Whitney stood up to her dad, I decided to take a stand too. I moved out and started supporting myself, and some people would say I have my priorities backward, but I chose to spend more money on the type of clothing I was used to than getting a reliable ride.

I'm starting to see that might have been a mistake.

The man finally pulls his gaze away from me and scans the area around us. "Yeah, you're not gonna get any reception out here. But don't worry, I can give you a ride to the nearest town. My bike should be able to carry all three of us."

I hesitate for a moment, my mind racing with all the potential dangers of getting on the back of a stranger's motorcycle. But then I remind myself that I'm in the middle of nowhere with a toddler, and I don't have any other options.

And for some inexplicable reason, I *know* deep down in my soul that this man would never hurt me or Maggie.

Is that crazy?

"Okay," I say, finally finding my voice. "Thank you so much."

He gives me a crooked smile, and I feel a flutter in my stomach. "No problem. Hop on."

I carefully lift Maggie onto the back of the motorcycle and then climb on behind her. The man revs the engine, and with a roar, we take off down the deserted road.

The wind whips through my hair, and I cling tightly to Maggie, feeling the heat of the man's body through his leather jacket.

As we speed down the road, I can't help but steal glances at him. He's ruggedly handsome with the wind tousling his dark hair.

I shake my head, trying to push away the strange attraction I feel toward him. After all, I don't even know his name.

But as we pull into the small town and he

helps me off the bike, I know that I want to know more about him.

"Thank you so much," I say, turning to face him. "I don't know what I would have done without you."

He smiles at me again, and I feel my knees go weak. "Don't mention it. Just happy to help."

"I still don't even know your name," I say, feeling emboldened.

He chuckles, a low and sexy sound that sends shivers down my spine. "It's Billy."

"Billy," I repeat, savoring the taste of his name on my tongue.

We stand there for a moment just looking at each other before he clears his throat. "Why don't you come on into my shop, and I'll fix you right up, doll?"

My heart flutters at the endearment.

"Sure—" I start and then pause. "Wait? *Your* shop?"

He grins at me, a rakishly handsome smile. "Yeah, I'm the owner of this place."

My eyes flick up to the sign.

Mayor's Mechanics.

"So, you're Billy Mayor?"

He smiles at me again, showing a full set

of white, even teeth. "The one and only, Jessie Cunningham."

My eyes widen when he says my last name, and I wrap an arm around Maggie and take a step back.

How does he know who I am?

CHAPTER
TWO

Billy

"WAIT. How do you know my full name? I didn't tell you my last name."

I internally curse myself for my slip-up.

Of course I know who Posh (Jessie Cunningham) is. Her father is one of the richest fuckers in the city, and I'll never forget the first time I saw the little brunette heiress.

She had to have been just sixteen. She was driving a pretty pink Corvette her father no doubt bought her. Her shoulder-length bob flowed in the wind, and her oversized sunglasses made her bee-stung lips stand out even more.

I was instantly *obsessed*.

I've been following her ever since, silently keeping an eye on her. I know it makes me sound like a creeper, but if I'm being honest, I was just waiting for her to turn eighteen.

Apparently, I'm a pussyfoot too because she's been eighteen for five years now. Jessie is twenty-three, and I already know that little girl she has with her is her best friend's—not hers.

Thank fuck.

You can bet your ass there was no way in hell I was going to let another motherfucker get near my girl and knock her up.

She's *mine*.

Mine to hold, mine to love, mine to *breed*.

It's hard to explain why I've waited so long to approach Jessie. Maybe it's that I've become so used to just watching her from afar. Maybe it's because the perfect opportunity never presented itself.

Christ, the girl is so far out of my league, it's ridiculous. No way in a million years will I ever be good enough for a girl as high class as her. She's the fantasy guys like me dream about.

And now here she is in my shop.

It's surreal. I'm convinced I'll wake up any minute and find that this is all a dream.

Jessie lifts a perfectly manicured hand and pulls her sunglasses up until they rest on top of her head, revealing big brown eyes that are even more enchanting up close in person like this.

I swallow, my gaze sinking into hers like quicksand. I clear my voice, but it still comes out rough as sandpaper when I try to play it cool.

"Everyone knows who Posh is."

Her eyes widen, and a pretty blush stains her cheeks.

"You know my dad?" she questions.

"I know of him," I state simply. Yeah, I don't know the fucker personally, but I know *of* him. Hell, who doesn't? Can't say I like the fucker, but I'm not going to tell Jessie that, though from what I've surmised over the years, she's lost touch with her old man too.

My chest swells with pride. Jessie might have grown up wealthy, but it's clear she's not a shallow princess. She was willing to give all that up to try to make her own way in the world when it came time to stand up for her principles.

I couldn't be prouder of her.

I can't tell her all that, though, without revealing that I've been keeping a close eye on her for years.

I'm sure that would freak her out—and it should.

I've accepted that there's something wrong with me. That this obsession with Posh is something that's eating me from the inside out.

And the fucked up thing about it is it's not something I care to fight.

It simply is what it is. It's not going away, and neither am I.

I'm going to be in Jessie's life one way or the other whether she realizes it or not. I pray to god I can be in her the life the way I want to. Me by her side forever.

But even if my girl doesn't want me that way, I'll still always watch over her. No one will ever hurt her on my watch.

"Let me call my tow truck guy and get him to haul your car over here, and then I'll give it a look."

Jessie glances at the clock over my shoulder and bites her lip. That juicy pink flesh giving way under her teeth like a ripe fruit is almost enough to make me groan, but I restrain myself even as I feel a bead of precum make its way up my cock and bubble from the tip.

"How long do you think it will take?"

"Not too long," I assure her, my eyes flicking to little Maggie. I already know why Jessie is nervous. She doesn't want her best friend's husband to find out about her getting stranded on the side of the road with his daughter. From what I've observed (I don't know the man personally), he's overly protective of his wife and daughter. Can't say I blame him. I'd be the same way about Jessie and our child.

My heart leaps in my chest at that thought as my eyes rake over Jessie, imagining it.

I can see Jessie's stomach rounded with my child now, the beautiful glow she'd have carrying our baby within her.

The jealous look on every man's face when they see her swollen belly and realize that *I'm* the one who put my seed in her.

Me and no one else.

My cock swells even harder in my pants. If it gets any harder, I might pass out from lack of blood flow to my brain.

Jessie's phone rings, and a panicked look overtakes her face when she looks at who's calling.

It's the little girl's parents, no doubt. Probably wondering where their child is.

"Um, yeah," Jessie stammers. "Well, you see, we ran into a little issue."

Jessie winces and holds the phone away from her ear as the girl's father apparently loses his shit.

The only reason I don't skin him alive for talking to my girl that way is because I know he means no disrespect, and he's completely enamored with his wife, Jessie's best friend.

Otherwise, he'd be a dead man.

"Fine," Jessie finally huffs out. "I'm at Mayor's Mechanics."

Jessie looks down at the little girl clinging to her hand when she hangs up the phone.

"Her dad is on his way to come get her," she tells me. "Which is probably for the best. She's probably ready to get home."

Maggie yawns sleepily, affirming Jessie's summation.

Just then, my tow guy pulls up with Jessie's car.

I guide him into my shop, feeling Jessie's eyes watching my every move.

I'm hyperaware of her presence. Every cell in my body is razored in on her, but I try to act normal and do my job.

I try not to get involved when Jon comes storming into my shop, his eyes frantically scanning the vicinity for his daughter.

He turns accusing eyes to Jessie, and I tense.

I might understand the guy's overprotectiveness, but that still doesn't mean I'll let him talk to her any kind of way.

So, he'd better watch himself.

Fortunately for him, he reigns it in, and I don't have to murder him. He even offers her a ride home, but she refuses.

My girl is too proud to go with him after he's ruffled her feathers, and I'm glad she doesn't.

The guy may be married, but that still doesn't mean I want him alone with my Jessie.

Everyone calls her Posh, but to me, she's Jessie. Because I see the *real* her. The her that she hides away from everyone else.

And I'm going to show her that she doesn't have to hide from me. She can always be herself around me, and I'll take care of her.

Fuck her father. I'm the only daddy my girl will ever need.

I blink, taken aback by the turn my thoughts have taken, but fuck it. The realization that that's just what I want to be to her settles over me.

I've never been into any particularly kinky fuckery, but something settles inside me.

Yeah, I'll be all the daddy Jessie Cunningham needs.

By the time I'm through with her, Jessie will be *mine*.

Heart, mind, body, and soul.

Just like I'm hers.

She just doesn't know it yet.

And that's why I'm every sort of bastard for fibbing about how long it's going to take me to fix her car.

After I close the hood, I wipe my hands on a rag and turn to her. "I'm going to have to keep it for at least a week."

Jessie's face falls. "A week?"

I nod. "I'm afraid so, doll."

She chews on that pretty, plump lip of hers again.

"What am I going to do without my car for a week?"

I pounce on the opportunity. "I can take you anywhere you need to go."

Her eyes flick to me in surprise. "Really? You don't mind?"

I almost laugh. Mind? An excuse to be in such close proximity to my obsession is like a wet dream come true.

"Not at all, beautiful."

Jessie's face heats as she smiles at me shyly, and my blood races beneath my skin.

Jessie Cunningham, you are *mine*.

CHAPTER
THREE

Posh

I KEEP PEAKING glances over at Billy. He's driving me home—in a car this time.

Part of me wishes he had taken the bike because then I'd be behind him with my arms wrapped around him. I'd have an excuse to press my body against his and smell his scent.

God, that makes me sound like such a creeper.

But then again, another part of me is glad we took the car because I can keep looking at his face.

I love his face.

He's the most handsome guy I've ever seen. Everything about him is just so...I don't know.

But it calls to something inside me.

I could happily sit next to Billy for the rest of my life.

That thought should scare me, but it doesn't.

It makes me feel warm and safe, like this is where I belong.

We chit-chat on the way to my apartment. I can't even exactly tell you what we talk about because we talk about anything and everything.

It feels like I've known him forever. He seems to understand me more than anyone I've ever known—aside from my best friend, Whitney.

It's like when Billy looks at me, he really sees *me*. Jessie Cunningham—not Posh.

That's why when we finally pull up at my apartment and Billy throws the car into park, I'm not ready for this to end.

"Do you want to come inside?" I blurt out before I can lose my nerve.

Billy looks surprised, but then his eyes

take on a heated look as they smolder at me. "I would love to, doll."

My cheeks heat at the endearment, and I decide that I'll never love anything more than hearing Billy Mayor call me "doll."

"I love it when you do that," Billy suddenly says, his voice husky.

My heart flutters in my chest as I stare up at him, my throat suddenly dry. "Do what?"

He reaches out and strokes his thumb over my cheek. "When you blush like that for me."

I can't speak. All I can do is stare up at him as he continues to stroke my cheek, his gaze roving over my face like he wants to commit it to memory.

Is this real? Can this really be happening?

I stare into his blue eyes that are blazing at me hotter than any flame.

We just stand there staring at each other, him stroking my cheek oh so tenderly until he finally pulls in a shaky breath and steps away from me, dropping his hand.

"Christ," he murmurs.

My face flames brighter, and I turn to open my door, suddenly embarrassed and wondering if I did something wrong. Hell, I probably looked like an idiot just standing there staring up at him. Was I supposed to do something? Say something?

I don't know because for all of my talk, I've never really been with a guy. I might be a shameless flirt, but I know relatively nothing about the opposite sex other than what I've read about in books.

We walk quietly into the building, and I unlock the door to my apartment and step inside.

"Would you like something to drink?" I offer, suddenly even more nervous.

He nods. "Yeah, a beer would be nice."

I nod and move to my small kitchen to grab us two beers. I hand him one and take a sip of mine, my gaze fluttering up to his.

I feel like I'm about to vibrate right out of my skin. I'm so nervous that I don't know what to do with myself—which is odd because I'm *never* nervous.

But Billy does something inexplicable to me.

Billy sets his beer down and walks over to me, his expression darkening with desire. Without a word, he clasps his hand around my waist and pulls me towards him. I gasp, feeling my body flush with heat as he leans in closer to me.

"I can't wait any longer," he murmurs, his voice low and husky. "I need to have you, doll."

My heart practically leaps out of my chest at his words. Is he really saying what I think he's saying?

Before I can even respond, he captures my lips in a searing kiss. His mouth is hot and demanding, his tongue sweeping in to tangle with mine. I moan into his mouth, my hands gripping onto his shoulders as he pulls me closer to him.

He breaks the kiss and stares down at me with darkened eyes. "I need you," he repeats, his voice thick with desire.

I nod, feeling a sudden surge of bravery. I want this too. I want him.

He picks me up effortlessly and carries me towards my bedroom, his lips trailing kisses down my neck and collarbone. I let out a breathy sigh, feeling my body pulse with pleasure at his touch.

When we reach my bed, he lays me down gently, his eyes never leaving mine. He takes off his shirt, revealing his toned and muscular chest. I can't help but stare as heat pools between my legs.

He leans down and captures my lips in another kiss, his hands trailing down my body to pull off my clothes. I'm naked beneath him, feeling vulnerable and exposed, but also incredibly aroused.

"So fucking perfect—just like I knew you would be," he says as his gaze roves over me before he proceeds to lick and kiss every inch of me.

I feel his hands shaking as they skate across my skin, and my own shake too as I touch him back, marveling at the cords of muscle rippling across his arms and chest.

"Fuck, Jessie," he finally groans as he shucks off his pants.

I gasp as I take in the sheer length and girth of him. The man is more than well endowed.

His cock is standing up straight and hard with moisture oozing from the tip. His veins are pronounced, and I can practically *see* him throbbing.

My own sex throbs in response.

He settles himself down on top of me. I

feel his tip prodding at my entrance, but he doesn't enter me yet.

Instead, he cups my face in his huge hands and stares into my eyes.

"You're mine from this moment on. Do you understand me, Jessie?"

I melt beneath him as I nod.

"No, I mean it, baby. Once I get inside you, that's it. I'm not one of those guys who can do things halfway. You. Are. Mine. I'm never letting you go. Do you get what I'm saying to you?"

My heart skips. Billy has a half-crazed look in his eyes, and maybe I'm crazy too for liking it.

It's like he's *obsessed* with me, and I feel a warm glow start inside me.

I *want* him to be obsessed with me.

I want him to want *me*.

Me and *only* me.

I reach up and take his face in my hands like he has mine as I whisper. "Yes, I understand. I'm yours, Billy."

He makes a strangled sound, and then he plunges into me without warning.

I gasp at the sting of the sudden intrusion. He groans and stills, giving me time to adjust to him. "Oh fuck, oh fuck, oh fuck," he chants before he begins to drop kisses all over my cheeks, my eyes, my forehead.

He makes me feel precious and adored.

He strokes his hands over my head and down my arms, touching me reverently, like he's worshipping me.

"My beautiful girl. So perfect. Daddy's perfect little angel."

My pussy clamps around him when he calls himself that forbidden word. It shocks me, but I can't say I dislike it.

No, judging by the moisture that floods between my legs, I fucking *love* it.

And I don't know why.

"Yesss," he hisses as he fists his hands in my hair and captures my eyes with his own. "You love that, don't you, baby? You love me calling myself your daddy? Makes this perfect little pussy so wet, doesn't it?"

All I can do is moan in response, and the sound must push Billy over the edge because he makes another strangled sound, and then he begins to thrust in and out of me.

I close my eyes and cry out, my back arching as his cock hits every single sensitive nerve inside of me.

When I start to claw at his back, he thrusts deeper and faster. "More, Daddy," I beg against his lips, my hands gripping his muscular ass.

"Oh fuck, Jessie, baby," he grunts as he redoubles his efforts, pounding into me even harder and faster than before.

I can feel my orgasm slowly rising with every thrust, my muscles tightening with each movement of his hips. He grunts and thrusts harder, increasing the pace with each second.

"Don't stop," I whisper, my head spinning with pleasure. "Don't stop, Daddy."

He growls, his eyes glazed over with need. He's on the verge of losing control, every muscle in his neck taut.

"You want Daddy to give you all he's got, little girl? Huh?" he grunts.

"Mmm-hmmm," I moan, lifting my hips up to him.

"Fuck," he growls as his thrusts become raw and fierce, almost violent. My orgasm comes without warning, my back arching as my pussy clenches tightly around his cock.

I moan out loudly, my body shaking with

pleasure. "Billy," I whisper, my voice breathy. "Oh god, Billy."

"Call me Daddy," he orders as he grips my neck. "Call me Daddy when I bust this big nut in you.

That sends a new wave of pleasure crashing down over me.

"Daddy!" I scream out as my next orgasm crashes over me like a tidal wave.

"Fuuuuck," he roars, and then he comes too. His cock spasms inside of me, his muscles tightening as he spills his warm cum into my wet pussy.

He kisses me deeply, wrapping his arms around my back and nearly lifting me off the bed with his kiss.

I release a long breath, my heart pounding in my chest.

"I love you," he whispers, his eyes locked on mine. "I love you with all my soul. I'm going to love you until the day I die and a hundred years after that."

My soul takes flight. This might be fast, but I don't care. I feel the truth of his words settle into me, and I can't deny my own truth.

"I love you too," I whisper back.

Billy's cock is still hard inside me, and I feel it jump at my confession.

He cups my face again, his eyes blazing down into mine as he affirms again, "I love you so fucking much. You'll never truly understand how much, Jessie."

I don't argue with him. Instead, I grab the back of his neck and pull him down to kiss him, trying to communicate to him with my lips what I can't seem to put into words.

And now I'm grateful as fuck for my piece of shit car breaking down on the side of the road.

I don't know how I lived my life before Billy, and I know now that I never want to live without him again.

CHAPTER
FOUR

Billy

I DON'T KNOW how I lived my life without Jessie. Watching her from afar all these years was a bittersweet torture, and now that I know what it's like to have her sunshine in my life, there is no way I could ever go back to watching her from the shadows.

I'm not trying to be dramatic or poetic here, but I really can't imagine going back to my former life.

It's like I was seeing everything in black and white before.

Now, everything is in vivid technicolor.

I know we're moving fast, but it still feels right.

I know Jessie feels the same way that I do.

I also know that in this situation, I'm pretty much fucked.

I don't know what I'd do if she were to tell me that she needed to "take a break." I've never wanted someone to stay in my life more than I want Jessie to stay in my life.

My obsession with her has been taken to a new level. Now that I've held her in my arms, there is no going back.

I'm insane when it comes to her. I glare at every man who even glances at her. Fuck every other male out there. I don't even want them looking at her.

She's *mine.*

Mine, mine, *mine.*

Even now that I've fixed her car, I still take her everywhere, and thank god she's okay with that. I drive her to her job at the interior design studio she works at. She works as an assistant to the primary designer, but I know that Jessie aspires to call the shots herself one day.

I want to make all her dreams come true,

and I've been saving most of my money for years in preparation of doing just that.

I'm just waiting for the right time to tell my girl that her daddy has all she needs for her to start her very own interior design company.

She can be her own boss, and she'll do amazing. I just know it. I have faith in my girl.

I'd have to say one of my favorite parts of every day is when I'm waiting there to pick her up after work. I love seeing the way her face lights up when she sees me.

I love the way she tries to walk like an adult, but then she can't help herself and ends up sprinting the rest of way and jumping right into my arms like the daddy's girl she is.

That's why I'm always waiting outside the car, leaning up against it. I love nothing more than to catch her up in my arms and feel her legs wrap around me as I claim her lips in a kiss like I haven't kissed her in a year.

It's always that way with us, though. We can have sex in the morning, and by the afternoon, we're already starving for each other again.

There are plenty of times we've barely

made it into the car before I had her straddling my lap and riding my dick like she's the star cowgirl in a rodeo show.

Jessie runs to me now, looking even more excited than usual.

A goofy grin overtakes my face as she leaps into my arms and squeals.

"Guess what, guess what, guess what?" she gushes as she peppers my face with kisses.

I chuckle as I hold her close to me. "What, doll?"

"I got offered a new job!" she squeals. "Mike is going to give me a promotion. He just wants me to meet him for dinner tonight to go over the details and see my portfolio I've been working on all these years."

I want to be happy for her, but I instantly tense. Mike is one of the higher-ups at the company she works for, and I disliked the fucker on sight.

Why?

Because all these years he's lusted after my Jessie. I see the salacious way he looks at her, and little does my Jessie know that the only reason she hasn't gotten this opportunity before was because of me.

I've purposefully done everything I could to keep this fucktard away from my girl.

But now he's finally managed a way to try to get close to her, and I'm not having it.

Over my dead body.

But how do I tell Jessie that without looking like a controlling bastard?

I set Jessie slowly on the ground, and she blinks up at me, instantly sensing that something's wrong.

"What is it?" she asks me.

"I just don't know if this is a good idea, doll."

Her face falls, and she takes a step back from me. "What? Why not? You know how hard I've worked and how much I've been wanting a break like this. How are you not happy for me?"

I hate the hurt I see on her face, and I hate even more knowing that it's me that put that look there, so I decide to go for honesty.

"Jessie, baby, that fucker Mike only wants in your pants."

Jessie's entire body instantly stiffens. "So, you don't think my work is good enough for me to be promoted on merit alone? If a man is promoting me, it's only because of my body right?"

I pass a hand over my face. "Jesus," I mutter, "that's not what I meant at all, Jessie. How can you even think that?"

But she's not hearing me. She shakes her head and backs away from me. "I don't need a ride today, Billy. In fact, it might be good for us to just cool things for a bit."

Panic instantly overloads my system. I take a step toward her. "Jessie, now wait a minute. Let's not overreact. You're not listening to me. That's not what I meant at all, baby."

But she's already walking away from me.

I race up behind her and spin her to face me. My voice is desperate, but I don't give a fuck. There's no use hiding how I feel from her.

She's my everything.

"You remember what I told you the first time we were together? You are *mine*, Jessie. Forever. I'm never letting you go."

My heart cracks when Jessie won't meet my eyes as she pulls away from me and says the words I've been dreading. "I just need some time, Billy. If you really love me, you'll respect that. I've never asked you for anything, but I'm asking you now."

I firm my jaw as I glare down at her. She still won't look at me, and I know damn well why.

It's because she can't. Because she knows deep down this is wrong. We aren't meant to be apart.

But how can I refute her words? If I force myself on her now, she'll always be able to say I didn't give her a choice.

So, I don't say another word. Instead, I simply stand there and watch her walk back into the building, taking my heart and soul with her.

If she wants a break, I'll give her the semblance of one.

But I'll still be there.

She's never getting rid of me.

When she calls, her daddy will come running.

CHAPTER FIVE

Posh

TEARS BRIM in my eyes as I go back into the building I work in. No use in going home with Billy. I might as well just stay here until it's time to meet Mike for dinner.

It stings that Billy doesn't have more faith in my interior design skills. Of all people, he is the one person who I thought would believe in me.

I try to ignore the ache in my chest as I get ready for the dinner. I'm going over my portfolio, making a few last-minute tweaks to make sure I'm showcasing my best work.

I can't think about Billy. Not now.

I take a cab to where I'm supposed to meet Mike.

I want to come across as confident and professional, but I can't be anything close to confident when my mind is filled with thoughts of the way Billy looked at me.

The hurt and worry in his eyes.

I walk into the restaurant and instantly spot Mike. He grins at me, and something about the look in his eyes makes my skin crawl.

I try to shake off the feeling. It's probably just Billy getting inside my head.

"Posh," Mike greets me, and I ignore the pang of hearing my nickname.

I've gotten so used to Billy calling me by my real name. If I really break up with Billy for good, will I ever hear anyone call me anything other than Posh again? Will anyone ever really see *me* again?

But then again, I thought Billy saw me, but he doesn't believe my work is good enough for me to get a promotion. He thinks it's all about my body.

"Come on, we've got a table," Mike tells

me. He moves to wrap his arm around my shoulder, but I panic and sidestep him.

I might not be happy with Billy at the moment, but that doesn't mean I want another man touching me.

I look around as we walk in, taking in the night club vibe of the place. My stomach drops. This isn't a standard restaurant. In fact, it's not the type of place I would imagine many business meetings are held in.

It seems too...seedy.

"So, Posh, tell me more about yourself," Mike says, his eyes raking over as we settle into our seats.

"About my work, you mean," I correct him as I pull out my portfolio.

Mike waves a hand dismissively. "Yes, yes, whatever you want to talk about, babe."

I cringe at the moniker. Billy never calls me "babe." It's always "doll" or "baby," and I don't like the way it sounds coming from Mike.

I pull out my portfolio and spin it to show it to him. I flip through a few of the pages, explaining my reasoning behind some of the designs I chose, trying my best to showcase my skills.

But Mike isn't looking at my designs.

I feel his gaze on me, and when I look up and meet his eyes, my heart falls.

He's looking at me like *I'm* what's on the menu tonight.

Billy was right.

My god, I'm such an idiot.

I'm *not* going to get a promotion by sleeping my way to the top.

As if reading my mind, Mike smirks. "No, I don't think I want to talk about your work, Posh. Or at least, not yet." He leans forward, his eyes trailing from my face down to my breasts and then farther down. He eyes my body slowly and intensely, and I can't help but squirm in my seat.

I try to tamp down the fear that's bubbling up within me.

It's not like he's going to throw me up against the wall and rip my clothes off.

I wish Billy was here. He would make this all better. I don't care if he didn't believe in me.

I need him.

Tears rush to my eyes, and I move to stand. "This was a mistake," I murmur, but then Mike's hand shoots out and bands around my wrist like a shackle.

And that's when all hell breaks lose.

Suddenly, Billy is there. I don't know where the hell he came from, but he's got Mike hauled up out of his seat faster than I can blink.

Billy is standing close to Mike, his face inches away from Mike's, and I can see the fire in his eyes as he glares at him. Mike flinches back, obviously intimidated by Billy's sudden outburst. I can feel my heart racing, and my body shaking. I didn't know Billy had it in him to be so violent. For a moment, I'm scared of him, but then he turns to me and takes my hand, pulling me up from my seat.

"Let's go, Jessie," he says, his voice deep and soothing, and I instantly relax at hearing him speak my real name.

I nod, grateful for his presence. As soon as we step out into the cool night air, Billy pulls me into his arms, holding me close to him. I can feel his chest rising and falling against mine, and I close my eyes, savoring the warmth of his embrace.

"I'm sorry, Jessie, baby," he whispers into my ear. "I'm so sorry. I shouldn't have let you walk away from me. I knew." His voice breaks. " I knew, and it's not that I didn't believe in you, honey. It's just that I knew what he was after. I'm sorry I wasn't there for you when you needed me."

I shake my head, tears streaming down my face. "It's not your fault, Billy," I say, my voice choked with emotion. "I should have known better than to trust Mike. I should have trusted you, and you were there when I needed you. If you hadn't come when you..." my voice catches on a sob as what could have happened finally hits me.

"Ssh," Billy quiets me. "Don't talk about it, baby. I'm here now, and I swear to you no one will ever hurt you, honey."

He pulls back to look at me, his hands cupping my face. "You don't have to do this alone, Jessie," he says, his voice low and intense. "I'm here for you. Always. That's why I wanted to tell you...I've been waiting for the right time to tell you."

I pull back and look up at him.

He takes a deep breath before he plunges on, "I've been stalking you for years, doll. Ever since you were sixteen years old, I've been infatuated with you. I knew then that you were the only girl for me. I've been waiting all this time, and then when your car broke down on the side of the world, it's like the universe had spoken. It was time for me to introduce myself to you.'

"And now that I know how amazing it is to have your real presence in my life, I can't imagine my life without you. I've been saving damn near everything I've made all these years for our life together. I know you grew up in a life of luxury, and I don't know if I'll ever be able to give you what you're used to, but I'm damn sure willing to try, baby. I'll work my fingers to the bone. I'll do anything you want me to do if you'll just be my wife.'

"I want it all with you. The life, kids, hell, even a dog if you want. And I want to make all your dreams come true. I've got money set aside just for you to start your own business, baby. And it's not because I don't believe in you but because I *do*.'

"You're amazing, Jessie. I don't know much about interior design shit, but even I can see you're the best, and you deserve everything your heart wants and more. You never have to work another day in your life if you don't want to. You know your daddy will always take care of you, but if doing this will make you happy, then I'll support you all the way."

All I can do is stare at Billy, slack-jawed after his monologue. Fresh tears rush to my eyes, but this time, they're not tears or sadness or anything but happiness.

I lean into him, wrapping my arms around his neck and kissing him fiercely. The passion between us is palpable, and I can feel the heat of his body against mine. He presses his lips against mine with equal force, and I can feel his arms tightening around me, pulling me even closer.

As we break apart, I look up at him with all the love I feel in my heart. I can't believe I ever doubted him. Maybe I should be mad about his confession that he's been watching me all these years. Maybe I should be freaked out.

But I'm not.

I *love* it.

I love that he's that obsessed with me.

"How did I ever get so lucky?"

Billy pulls me even closer, his voice husky with emotion. "I'm the lucky one, Jessie. And I'll make sure that you're always happy and taken care of, baby. I love you more than anything in this world."

"I love you too, Billy," I reply, my heart swelling with emotion.

As we embrace again, I can feel the world around us melt away, leaving only the two of us in a whirlwind of passion and love. It's as if we're the only people on the planet, and nothing else matters but the connection we share.

"Thank you, Daddy," I tell him.

His eyes heat as he gazes down at me. "Anything for my good little girl."

My heart skips a beat at the look in his eyes.

I'll never tire of seeing that look of obsession on his face.

And I'll always be his good little girl.

EPILOGUE

One Year Later

Billy

I PLACE a hand on my wife's pregnant belly, my chest swelling with pride.

Yeah, motherfuckers, *I* did that. I fucked my child into her belly, and you can all eat your hearts out.

We're in my shop, and I can see all the men glancing over at my wife, though they're trying to be surreptitious about it.

I refrain from murdering them because

she's in *my* arms, and she's made it clear to everyone I'm her daddy.

I'm sure I'm biased, but I think Jessie is even more beautiful in her pregnancy. She really does have a happy glow about her, and I'm more ravenous for her now than ever.

But I think I'll always be like that with her. Instead of calming down, my obsession with her only grows stronger every day.

My cock is getting hard right now just looking at her.

She tilts her head up to smile at me, and I start leaking precum.

And that's just what I'm talking about. All Jessie has to do is *smile* at me, and I'm ready to nut.

I'm crazy for this girl.

Jessie reaches back behind her and palms my cock through my leather pants.

I hiss in a breath and grab her hand, pulling her into the garage I keep my motorcycle locked in. There's no one else in here, and I can't wait any longer.

"Naughty girl," I rasp in her ear as I bend her over the back of my motorcycle and pull up her maternity dress. "I think my little girl is wanting her daddy to fuck her."

I move my hand between her legs, my head spinning when I find out she's not wearing panties.

"Oh fuck, yes, you want it, don't you, baby? That's why you're not wearing any panties. Wanted to make sure there was nothing between Daddy and his pussy, didn't you?"

"Billy," Jessie moans as I rub her wetness all around her clit, stroking her just the way I know she likes. My girl loves it when I dirty talk her, and I'm always willing to give her whatever she wants.

"That's right," I grunt when she grinds her ass back against my cock. "You love your Daddy's cock, don't you, baby?"

Jessie is whimpering, squirming against me as I play with her.

"You're so wet, my bad little girl," I growl as I push two fingers inside her. I use my other hand to pet her clit, and Jessie throws her head back and moans my name.

"Yes, Billy. Daddy, please, fuck me," she whimpers, and I love that I've got her so worked up.

I love it when I can get her to moan, cry, scream, and everything else I want to hear.

"That's it, baby. Daddy's going to fuck you hard. Do you want that? Do you want Daddy to give you what you need?"

"Billy, please," she begs, the desperate note to her voice almost sending me over the edge.

I fall to my knees and lick her from behind, my tongue sliding along her pussy lips, licking up all her sweet nectar. God, I fucking love the way she tastes.

I use my fingers to spread her lips open, and I begin to lick her incessantly, flicking my tongue all over her while she moans my name over and over. Her hands grip onto the seat of the bike tightly as I lick her for all I'm worth, taking care of my little girl so she knows that more than anything I'm her everything.

My cock is hard as a rock, and I'm dying to fuck her. My cock is so fucking hard that I can feel precum dripping down it. It's continuously oozing from my tip, and I've got my hands wrapped around my shaft, stroking it for all I'm worth as I lick my wife's amazing pussy.

But I have to stop because I know that if I keep it up, I'm going to explode.

And I can't have that because I need to please her. I need to give her this big daddy dick until she's coming so hard on me she can't see straight.

"Good girl," I praise her as I push her forward until she's bending over the bike. "Daddy's little girl is so obedient for him. You want Daddy to bend you over and fuck you, don't you?"

She nods wildly, and I hold her ass with one hand while I position my cock with the other.

"Daddy's getting ready to give you what you've been asking for. Are you ready for Daddy's cock?"

"Yes," she moans. "Please, Billy, give me your cock."

I'm not wasting any time because I want to feel my cock buried in her as far as it can go. I slowly push my cock into her and begin to fuck her.

I want to come at the same time she does.

When I'm all the way in, I hold it there before I begin to slowly pull out. I slide back in, holding it there again before I pull out. She's moaning, clawing at the seat. Fuck, she's such a good girl for me.

I continue to slowly fuck her, my hands gripping her hips, rolling them back and forth as I plunge into her over and over. Both my hands go to her ass, and I spread her cheeks wide as I plunge into her. I love watching my cock slide in and out of her. I can see her juices dripping down my cock, and it's the most erotic thing in the world.

My balls slap against her pussy, and I can feel her tightening around my cock. I know she's close. She's so close she's trembling, and I can feel her coming all over me as she screams, altering between my name and "daddy."

I fucking love it. I'm the only one who's ever going to make her feel this way.

"Mine," I growl as I slam into her harder.

She moans louder, and I speed up, fucking her faster and faster. It's all I can do to hold back because I want to fill her with my cum. I want to come deep inside my little girl, but I don't want her to feel the cum leaving my cock just yet. I want to feel her pussy gripping me as my cum seeps into her tight little hole.

When I can feel her pussy tightening around me again, I finally allow myself to let go.

I hold tight onto her hips as I barrel up inside her one final time, throwing my head back and roaring as my release starts to travel up my stalk.

I can feel her pussy milking my cock, and she's screaming my name and calling me daddy as I begin to empty my load directly into her.

She's whimpering and twitching, and my cock keeps spasming inside her, dumping rope after rope inside her until it's dripping down our legs between us.

Fuuuck. Good thing she's already pregnant or that load would have for sure knocked her up.

When I finally pull out of her, I'm careful to catch her before she falls.

I cradle her in my arms and kiss her forehead gently.

"I love you, Jessie. You're my everything, you know that?"

"Yes, Daddy," she smiles up at me like a contented kitten, and my chest swells.

My perfect little girl. My wife. My life. My love.

My *everything.*

. . .

Want more Emma Bray? Go to www. authoremmabray.com to sign up for Emma's newsletter and get a free book!

Keep reading for a sample of The Trucker's Obsession!

Chapter 1

Blake

I pull into the truck stop and put my big rig into park. I sigh and wipe a heavy hand across my brow before I lean my forearms on my steering wheel and look out my windshield.

I can feel the silence of the truck stop, interrupted only by the rumble of my engine as it slowly fades away. The parking lot is empty but for the occasional car and truck, but nothing is moving. It's like no one is here, but I know there are plenty of other truckers here too. They're just probably all asleep in the backs of their rigs.

The sun is setting, casting long shadows across the highway and the parking lot. The dull hum of the buzzing fluorescent lights spills into the air, creating a strange sense of eeriness. The silence is so thick it feels like a blanket, enveloping me in its embrace. I can feel it, like a heavy weight pressing down on me.

There is something hauntingly beautiful about this moment, something that stirs a deep longing inside me. I don't know what it is or why it is so strong, but I can feel it in my bones. The stillness, the solitude, the absolute quiet. I find myself yearning to be part of it, to exist in this moment for just a little while longer.

I reach up and turn off the engine, plunging me into complete silence. The only sound I can hear now is my own breathing, and it's the only thing that I can focus on. I take a few deep breaths, and it feels like I am finally able to relax. I let my head rest on the headrest and close my eyes, taking in the peacefulness of the moment.

The dull hum of the fluorescent lights has

become a melody in my ears, and I can feel the entire truck stop like an extension of my own body. I take it all in, from the way the asphalt shimmers in the fading light to the way the shadows seem to stretch out for miles.

I feel the loneliness.

It is a feeling I know all too well, the heavy burden that comes from feeling completely alone. The sun is almost gone now, and the sky is a soft, fading shade of blue.

I exhale another breath and reach for the handle of my truck.

And then I go completely still.

My heart starts beating in overdrive, and every muscle in my body tightens when I see her.

I don't have a clue who she is, but she's the prettiest little thing I've ever seen in all my thirty-two years.

She's an angel.

No, she's a *goddess*.

Her long, red hair flows down over a backpack to an impossibly tiny waist. It's wild and untamed, like a lion's mane. She can't be more than five-foot-four and thin, but she still has a nice handful of curves.

She's nothing short of glorious.

But what the fuck is she wearing?

My cock is a rod of steel as my eyes sweep over her from head to toe. Her white tank top doesn't completely cover her stomach, leaving the expanse of skin just below her belly button and between the hem of her shorts exposed.

And *fuuuck*, those shorts.

They shouldn't even be allowed to be called shorts. They barely cover her ass, and while I'm loving the view, I'm instantly, irrationally enraged and jealous at the thought of other men seeing her like this.

And I know that's insane when I don't even know her.

My insanity goes up a notch when I see several men's heads turn in her direction as she makes her way to the door of the truck stop.

A low growl bubbles up in my throat when I see them blatantly checking her out.

I panic when I see some of them starting to follow her.

Jesus, she's going to start a riot if she's not

careful. I see the looks in their eyes. They're thinking the same thing I am, but the difference is I want to take care of her.

I want to be her protector.

And I make my decision here and now.

I fling open the door of the truck and cast threatening glances at every man following her.

She is *my* woman.